Joe Camp's Benji™
Meet Benji

By Scout Driggs & Kathleen Camp
Photos by Tony Demin
Based on the screenplay by Joe Camp

HarperKidsEntertainment
An Imprint of HarperCollinsPublishers

Meet Benji.

He is not your average dog.

He is not like any dog you have ever met.

From his first *"woof,"*

Benji knew he was different.

He is a beautiful golden color.

But his brothers and sisters have

pure black fur, just like their mom.

The only dark fur on Benji

is on the tips of his ears.

Mr. Hatchett, Benji's owner,
sold only black puppies—
the ones that looked like their mom, Daisy.
Mr. Hatchett did not want a golden puppy.

He took Benji's family away.

He left the tiny puppy all alone

in an old abandoned house.

Benji was sad, afraid, and lonely.

But not for long.

Thump, thump came sounds

from the porch.

"Puppy, puppy, where are you?"

It was Benji's friend, Colby!

Colby picked Benji up.

He snuggled the puppy inside

his warm jacket.

Then they left the empty house together.

Colby carried Benji to his secret fort.

He knew that Benji would be safe there.

When Colby and Benji entered the fort
they heard a screech.

"*Uhhh, ohhh!*" called a fluffy white bird.

"Meet Merlin," Colby said to the puppy.

"*Woof,*" replied Benji.

Colby told Merlin to watch over Benji
and to keep him out of trouble.
But Benji was curious and liked to explore.
It was going to be hard for Merlin
to keep Benji out of trouble!

Every day Colby visited the fort.

Benji and Merlin always waited patiently.

Colby brought them special treats.

He even brought Benji's mother to visit.

Colby made a special puppy pen

for Benji to sleep in.

Colby wanted Benji to stay

in the puppy pen so he would be safe.

But Benji didn't always want to

sleep in the pen.

Sometimes he wanted to sleep near

his new bird friend, Merlin.

Sometimes he did not want to sleep at all.

Sometimes he also wanted to explore.

Every day after Colby visited,

Benji climbed out of the pen.

It was a lot of work for a little puppy.

"*Uhhh, ohhh,*" screeched Merlin.

He knew Benji was sure to get in trouble.

Time went on.

Benji liked living in the fort.

He lived there for a long time.

He liked Merlin, too.

They became good friends.

As Benji grew, so did his curiosity.

He wanted bigger adventures.

Benji wanted to see

what was *outside* of the fort.

But Colby wanted Benji to stay *inside* the fort.

He was afraid Mr. Hatchett might find Benji and hurt him.

One afternoon when he thought Merlin wasn't looking, Benji snuck outside.

"*Stay, puppy. Stay!*" screeched Merlin.

"*Uhhh, ohhh!*"

Merlin flew off his perch, following Benji.

When Colby visited the fort that day,

it was empty.

Merlin and Benji were gone!

Colby was worried and sad.

Then he heard a familiar scratching and squawking coming from outside.

Merlin and Benji had returned safely.

They were all happy to be together again.

But while Merlin and Benji

were playing outside,

Mr. Hatchett had spotted them.

And now he was outside the fort,

watching!

"Where have you two been?"

Colby asked.

He did not know that Mr. Hatchett

was standing behind him.

"Who is this?" screamed Mr. Hatchett.

He was pointing at Benji.

Then he tried to grab Benji!

"*Uhhh, ohhh,*" said Merlin.

(He says that a lot.)

"No! You leave him alone," yelled Colby, pushing Mr. Hatchett away.

Mr. Hatchett didn't listen.

He tried to grab Benji again!

Benji raced through the door

and off into the woods.

He ran straight for the old house

where he was born.

It was the only safe place he knew.

Benji scratched at the house's big door with his paw.

Then he nudged it open with his nose.

Once inside, he sniffed the familiar air.

The smell reminded Benji of his mom.

Benji missed his friends and the fort.

He missed his mom, too.

But he would not be away for long.

Benji would be gone long enough
to figure out how to get Mr. Hatchett
out of their lives forever.

Benji is not your average dog!